Say Hello, Vanessa

by Marjorie Weinman Sharmat

illustrated by Lillian Hoban

SCHOLASTIC BOOK SERVICES
NEW YORK · TORONTO · LONDON · AUCKLAND · SYDNEY · TOKYO

ISBN 0-590-31583-8

Text copyright © 1979 by Marjorie Weinman Sharmat. Illustrations copyright © 1979 by Lillian Hoban. All rights reserved. This edition is published by Scholastic Book Services, a division of Scholastic Magazines, Inc., 50 West 44th Street, New York, N.Y. 10036, by arrangement with Holiday House, Inc.

12 11 10 9 8 7 6 5 4 3 2   0 1 2 3 4 5/8

Printed in the U.S.A.

For Margery and John

Vanessa Mouse lived with her mother and father on three floors of a fine, old house.

Mrs. Mouse had many friends. When they came to visit, Vanessa hid under the sofa and peeked out.

"Say hello, Vanessa," said her mother.

But Vanessa didn't.

When Mr. Mouse's friends came over, Vanessa sat in a corner and didn't look up.

"Look up, Vanessa," said her father.

But Vanessa wouldn't.

No friends came over to see Vanessa. Because Vanessa didn't have any.

"Not one friend," said Mrs. Mouse sadly. "Not even a now-and-then friend. Or an every Sunday friend. Or a rainy day, sit-by-the-window-and-nibble-crumbs friend. Nobody."

"Trying to make friends must be the scariest thing in the world," said Vanessa.

"Well, the first time might be a little scary," said Mrs. Mouse. "But why don't you try it?"

The next day Vanessa went to school. She took her seat in class behind Quincy Moose.

"It's wonderful hiding here behind Quincy Moose's antlers," thought Vanessa.

Mr. Mitchell, the teacher, said, "Today we'll start with spelling."

He looked at Andrew Aardvark. "Andrew, how do you spell country?"

"Does it begin with a *k*?" asked Andrew.

"No, I'm afraid it doesn't," said Mr. Mitchell. He looked at Craig Badger. "Can you spell country, Craig?"

"Does it end with an *e*?" asked Craig.

"No," said Mr. Mitchell, "it doesn't. Who knows how to spell country?"

Vanessa started to raise her hand. "I know how, I know how," she said to herself. Then she lowered her hand. "But I can't. Everybody will look at me and my funny teeth and my furry face. Maybe I'll spell country tomorrow."

After class, everyone got together in little bunches and groups. Except Vanessa who was all alone.

"Bunches and groups, bunches and groups," thought Vanessa. "Everybody has enough friends already. They don't need me."

When she got home, her mother asked, "Well, Vanessa, did you make a friend today?"

"No," said Vanessa. And she told her mother about bunches and groups.

"I understand," said Mrs. Mouse. "But if you look hard enough, you'll find someone who is alone. Then you can go up and say hello."

"I'll try that," said Vanessa.

At school the next morning, Mr. Mitchell asked, "Who has learned to spell country?"

Everyone looked around.

"Here's a chance that might never come again," thought Vanessa.

Vanessa started to raise her hand. But she put it down again. "Maybe tomorrow I'll do it," she thought.

When class was over, Vanessa saw Lisa Goat standing alone against a wall.

Slowly Vanessa went up to Lisa. Then Vanessa whispered, "Hello."

"What?" asked Lisa.

"Hello," whispered Vanessa.

"What?" asked Lisa again.

Vanessa walked away.

She ran home to her mother. "I said hello but I didn't make a friend," said Vanessa.

"Saying hello usually works," said Mrs. Mouse.

"It didn't for me," said Vanessa. "I went up to Lisa Goat very politely and said hello, just like that, but all she said was *what?*"

"Try again tomorrow with someone else," said Mrs. Mouse. "And speak a little louder."

"I'll try," said Vanessa.

Vanessa hurried to school the next morning and took her seat behind Quincy Moose.

Mr. Mitchell asked, "Who can spell country?"

"Me!" shouted Andrew Aardvark.

"I can, too," said Craig Badger.

"C-o-u-n-t-r-y!" someone else spelled.

"Nuts!" thought Vanessa. "Well, anyway, the day isn't over yet."

Vanessa walked up and down the hall looking for someone who was alone. At last she saw Sigmund Toad counting the pencils in his pencil pouch.

Vanessa walked up to him. "HELLO!" she shouted.

Sigmund dropped his pencil pouch.

"HELLO!" she shouted again.
Sigmund put his hands over his ears and hopped away.

That night Vanessa told her mother about her new hello.

"Maybe a medium hello will work," said Mrs. Mouse.

"I don't want to try any more hellos," said Vanessa.

The next day Vanessa's mind was made up. "Today I will not say anything. Not anything at all!" she said to herself.

She took her seat behind Quincy Moose.

"This morning we have a new word to spell, and it's a difficult one," said Mr. Mitchell. "Does anyone know how to spell tooth?"

"Oh!" thought Vanessa. "I do! I know that word!"

Mr. Mitchell looked around.

Andrew was squirming in his seat. Craig was pulling on his ear.

Vanessa felt hot and thumpy inside. She was thinking, "Tooth is such a great word to know how to spell, and *I* know how to spell it!"

Suddenly Vanessa raised her hand high. And higher. She wiggled it. She waved it. She said, "I can spell tooth! I can spell it! T-o-o-t-h!"

"Perfect," said Mr. Mitchell.

Everyone was looking at Vanessa. But she didn't
mind. In fact she felt good.

After class was over, Vanessa gathered up her books.

Suddenly Quincy Moose turned around. "I wish I knew how to spell tooth," he said. "I wish I knew how to spell moose."

"Moose is easy," said Vanessa. "It's like mouse except it has an *o* where the *u* is."

Vanessa and Quincy walked out of class together.

They sat on a bench and talked about *mouse* and *moose*.

"That was fun," said Quincy. "Let's do it again."

"Want to come to my house?" asked Vanessa.

"Sure," said Quincy.

Vanessa and Quincy walked to Vanessa's house.

They passed Mr. Mitchell.

"Hello, Mr. Mitchell," said Vanessa.

They passed Andrew Aardvark.

"Hi there, Andrew," said Vanessa.

They passed Craig Badger.

"How are you, Craig?" said Vanessa.

They passed Lisa Goat.

"Greetings, Lisa," said Vanessa.

They passed Sigmund Toad.

"Nice day, Sigmund!" said Vanessa.

When Vanessa got home, she ran into the house.

"Mother! Mother! I brought someone home!"

"I'm Quincy Moose. M-o-o-s-e," said Quincy. "And you must be Mrs. Mouse. M-o-u-s-e."

"And you must be Vanessa's friend," said Mrs. Mouse.

"That's who I am!" said Quincy.

"A friend is fun to have," said Vanessa. "Especially an everyday, sit-by-the-fire-and-talk friend."